AF470474

MOONGLOW

'Out of the air in front of him, a shape appeared, first thin and vague, then slowly firm and real, real and golden, the horse, Moonglow.'

It is purely by chance that Nick visits old Mr O'Hanlon. But if it hadn't been for this visit, he would never have found out about Moonglow — a Palomino horse so beautiful she seems fashioned from moonlight. He would also never have witnessed the delicate relationship formed many years ago between a young man and a beautiful spirited horse — a relationship that now, many years later, can only be sustained through dreams . . .

Thriller Firsts is an exciting series of fast-paced stories especially for younger readers of the seven to nine year age group. With clear, straightforward text and plenty of illustrations, readers are sure to be gripped.

David Wiseman was born in Manchester and attended both the grammar school and university there. After serving in the forces, he became a teacher and then a headmaster in Cornwall, where he still lives. He spends much time writing, painting and travelling.

Other titles in the series

Trick or Treat?	Jon Blake
Jumping Jack	David Wiseman
The Raft	Alison Morgan
The Creature in the Dark	Robert Westall
Scent of Danger	Rosemary Hayes
A Summer Witching	Andrew Matthews
Frog	Anthony Masters
Roboskool	Jon Blake
Secret Corridor	John Gordon
Take A Good Look	Jacqueline Wilson

David Wiseman

Illustrated by Tizzie Knowles

Blackie

For Mark

British Library Cataloguing in Publication Data
Wiseman, David *1916–*
Moonglow
I. Title II. Knowles, Tizzie III. Series
823′.914 J
ISBN 0-216-92860-5

Blackie and Son Ltd
7 Leicester Place
London WC2H 7BP

Printed in Great Britain

Chapter One

Nick Williams heard horses trotting past and went to the window. They were from the riding school down in the valley.

'They're beautiful aren't they?' He hadn't heard his friend Anna come in.

'They're all right, I suppose,' he said. Anna was mad on horses. She went to the riding stables whenever she could, got free rides in exchange for help with the mucking out. Nick thought she was silly. There were much better things to do with your time.

Anna lived in the house next door. The houses were on a council estate built twenty years before, set high up on the edge of the town. At the end of their gardens there were open fields. At the end of the Williams's garden Nick's father had put in a gate leading to the fields.

Sometimes the horses from the riding stables were brought to the fields to graze. Anna was always pleased at that. Nick could not see why. Horses were only horses, nothing special.

He heard his mother calling. She had been making biscuits and wanted Nick to take some to old Mr O'Hanlon.

'He's very fond of my biscuits,' she said.

Mr O'Hanlon lived in a house on the other side of the fields and it was possible to get to it by walking across the fields, but that meant jumping over a stream and climbing over farm gates.

Nick's mother, who had been a nurse, helped look after Mr O'Hanlon. He was very

old. Nick thought he must be a hundred, but his mother said that was nonsense.

'He's only eighty-five. It's just that he's had a hard life.'

Nick was a bit afraid of the old man and was not too sure he wanted to take the biscuits on his own. He'd only been to visit him with his mother before.

'He won't bite, except the biscuits,' his mother said with a laugh. 'It will do him the world of good to see a young face. Are you going with him, Anna?'

'Oh, no,' Anna said firmly. 'I'm off to the stables,' and, before Mrs Williams could say anything more, Anna had gone.

'Well!' Mrs Williams said. 'How about that?'

'She's mad about horses,' Nick explained.

'Then Mr O'Hanlon's the very man to see. Get him to tell you about them, about the old days. And wrap up against the wind. It's blowing hard. And go by the road, not the fields.'

As Nick walked along he had to bend his head against the wind. Twigs and leaves sped

past him. A sudden gust almost blew him back home, but he struggled on until, breathless, he reached Mr O'Hanlon's house. The old man's housekeeper, Mrs Thomas, showed him upstairs.

'I'll just give him the biscuits and leave,' Nick told her but when he saw Mr O'Hanlon, propped up in a chair, with a blanket round his knees, looking sadly out of the window, Nick felt sorry for him.

Mr O'Hanlon turned and his eyes shone with pleasure when he saw Nick.

'Ah, Nick,' he said. His voice was not at all

that of a frail old man, but strong and cheerful, with a musical lilt to it. 'It's grand to see you, so it is, and kind of your mother to think of me.' He took the tin of biscuits and put it on a table beside him. 'I'll enjoy these later but now 'tis you I'm glad to see.'

Nick hadn't been in the old man's bedroom before. He looked around. The walls were covered with pictures of horses.

The old man was talking. 'Sit down there, on the other side of the window, where I can see you.' Nick decided there was nothing at all frightening about the old man. His face was jolly, with his bright eyes and warm smile.

'So,' the old man said. 'What have you to tell me?'

What was there to tell? Nothing exciting ever happened. He racked his brains to think of something.

'I was nearly blown off my feet coming here,' he said.

'Why sure and it's wild wild weather we're having, it is,' Mr O'Hanlon said. 'But I've known worse. And it'll blow itself out. It always does. But while it lasts it may do a

terrible load of harm.' He opened the tin of biscuits and offered it to Nick.

'I shouldn't. They're for you,' he said.

'I can't eat on my own,' said the old man. 'Go on. I won't tell your mother.'

Nick took a biscuit. Mr O'Hanlon smiled and pushed the tin nearer to Nick so that it was within easy reach. Then he said slowly, 'Yes, it will blow itself out, so it will. But, before that . . .' He stopped and the sad look came back. At last he went on. 'I remember a storm of storms, a hurricane rather, tore up trees, ripped off roofs, sent chimney pots tumbling, and very nearly brought ruin to the O'Hanlons.'

Nick absent-mindedly reached for another biscuit.

'Do you know what I was in my young days?' the old man said. 'Ringmaster in a circus. My own circus, O'Hanlon's Family Circus. We travelled all over England and Ireland, here, there and everywhere. And it was here, in Kenwyn, this very town, that it happened.' He reached for a biscuit and bit into it. 'They're good these. You must tell your mother so. And help yourself.'

Nick took another biscuit. 'What happened?' he said.

'The hurricane. Over fifty years ago it was and I remember it as if it was yesterday. 'Twas terrible. The only time O'Hanlon's Circus had to close before the show was over. We had to set to and take the Big Top down before the wind took it.' He looked at Nick to see he understood. 'You know what the Big Top is, I suppose?'

'The circus tent?' Nick wasn't sure.

'Massive thing it was, too. Took every man

jack and woman of us to hold it and lots of helpers from the audience. A struggle we had, but we did it. Sad though, not to finish the show. And sadder still . . .' He turned his face from Nick and wiped his eyes before looking back. 'That's enough of that,' he said. 'What about you?'

But Nick couldn't think of anything to tell. Nothing exciting ever happened to him.

'I should be getting back,' he said.

'Tell your mother how good the biscuits were.' Mr O'Hanlon winked.

'I'll say you enjoyed them.' He realised he'd eaten three or four while Mr O'Hanlon had had only one.

'And come and see me again if you can spare the time,' the old man said.

'I promise,' Nick replied.

As he walked home, the wind was behind him, still blowing strongly but not a hurricane. Mr O'Hanlon said the hurricane had happened here, in Kenwyn. Nick wondered where the circus field had been.

'He said to say thank you for the biscuits,' he told his mother later. 'He said to tell you

how good they are.'

'Did he tell you about his horses?'

'No. Just about the hurricane that made them stop the show. I didn't know he had a circus.'

'That was a long time ago, but people still talked about it when I was a little girl. They all remembered the night the Big Top came down.'

'Where was it? The circus field?'

'Why, here, where these houses are. I thought everyone knew. Too windy for pitching a tent, but not too windy to build houses.' She sounded a bit cross.

'What about the horses?' Nick said.

'I'll leave him to tell you that. It's his story. It upsets him sometimes, but he'll get round to it I expect, when you see him again. You will go and see him again, won't you?'

'Oh, yes. I'd like to know about the circus.'

Chapter Two

Nick was curious to know about circus life and he went to see Mr O'Hanlon as often as he could. The old man kept him amused with tales of life on the road.

'How old are you, Nick?' he said once.

'Eleven,' Nick said, then added, 'Well, I will be next birthday.'

'I went everywhere with the circus when I was your age, got my schooling anywhere on the way. It was a hard life, believe you me, not all fun and frolics.'

Though Mr O'Hanlon was full of stories of the men and women he worked with — Samson, the lion-tamer, the Bordinos, the trapeze artists, and Chief Sitting Bull, the knife-thrower — he never mentioned horses.

'He will tell you one day, I'm sure,' Nick's mother said.

But for several weeks after that, Nick did not see Mr O'Hanlon, for the old man was taken ill with pneumonia and was not well enough to have visitors. Then, one day towards the end of July, Nick's mother said, 'Mr O'Hanlon was wondering if you would go and see him. He's a lot better now.'

This time the old man was in bed, sitting up against the pillows. He was reading but when Nick went in he peered over his glasses and put his book aside.

'So,' he said. 'Were you nearly blown off your feet this time? It's not blowing a gale today. It's warm and sunny. Ah sure, those were the best days of all, the sun shining high in the sky and people coming from all the villages around to see us. Everyone cheerful. Have you noticed that? The sun makes the whole world smile, so it does.'

He looked even older than before, his hair whiter, his face more wrinkled, but he had the same bright eyes and the same welcoming smile. 'Mind you,' he said, 'it could get very hot and sticky under the Big Top. The clowns grumbled, so they did, but then the clowns were a grumpy pair. They were my brothers, Seamus and Sean. Gone now, poor fellows. Never got over the circus closing. Joined

another one but 'twasn't the same. There was
only one O'Hanlon's.'

For a long time he was quiet then, and lay
back with his eyes closed. Nick thought perhaps he had gone to sleep and wondered if he
should creep away. Then the old man opened
his eyes and looked sharply at him.

'Horses? Do you like them?' he suddenly
asked.

'Sort of,' Nick said.

'Know anything about them?'

'Not much.'

'They were my life, to be sure, my own, my special thing.' He waved his hands towards the pictures on the walls of his room. 'There, that's what we were famous for. O'Hanlon's Equestrian Ballet. I grew up with horses, in Ireland. They tell me I could ride before I could walk. Never knew a bad horse yet. Maybe there are such but I never met one. It's how you treat them. I remember one . . .' He paused and his voice drifted away. Nick waited.

'Ring the bell,' the old man said. Nick rang the handbell on the table beside the bed.

Mrs Thomas came in answer, clicked her tongue in irritation, went up to the bed and straightened the bed covers.

'Stop fussing, will you now,' the old man said impatiently. 'Bring some of Mrs Williams's biscuits. This lad has a hunger on him. His mother's baking works wonders.'

Nick felt guilty but Mrs Thomas smiled as if she understood.

'And bring that scrapbook, of the old circus.' Mrs Thomas folded her arms and did not move. 'Please,' said the old man and Mrs

Thomas nodded her head and went away.

'She treats me like a child, she does,' the old man grumbled. 'With her please and thank you.'

'It is more polite,' Nick said.

Mr O'Hanlon grinned at him. 'Don't you start. I like my bit of grumble.'

Mrs Thomas came back with a plate of biscuits and a large black book. She made another effort to tidy the bed before leaving. As soon as she had gone Mr O'Hanlon loosened the covers she had so carefully arranged. 'I hate having tight sheets. I have to feel free.'

Nick felt differently. He loved his mum or dad tucking the bedclothes round him at night. It gave him such a safe feeling.

'Pull your chair near,' Mr O'Hanlon said. 'And have a look at this.' He picked up the big black book and passed it to Nick. The effort seemed to tire him for he sighed and lay back on his pillows while Nick turned the pages.

There were cuttings from newspapers, photographs of trapeze artists and clowns, handbills advertising O'Hanlon's Family Circus, and a large poster folded to fit into the book.

O'HANLON'S
Renowned & Never-To-Be-Forgotten
EQUESTRIAN BALLET
featuring
MOONGLOW
Beauty & Grace
combined in an
ACT BEYOND COMPARE
O'HANLON BROTHERS
moonglo

Nick opened it up and read 'O'Hanlon's Renowned and Never-To-Be-Forgotten Equestrian Ballet, featuring Moonglow. Beauty and Grace combined in an Act beyond Compare.'

He stole a glance at Mr O'Hanlon but his eyes were closed and Nick didn't want to disturb him. He turned the pages of the scrapbook and saw a picture from a newspaper. It showed a troupe of horses bowing before a frock-coated man. It was Mr O'Hanlon, a young man but the same. His hair was dark and crowned his head just as his white locks did now. He stood, raising a long whip, while the ten black horses bowed to the ground at his command. But one horse in front of the others reared up on its hind legs, as if refusing to bow. It stood proudly upright, its colour in contrast to the black of the others, its mane and tail white, its coat light and glossy.

There was something special about the horse and, from Mr O'Hanlon's secret smile in the photograph, something special about his feeling for it. Nick wanted to know more, but the old man was asleep. Gently Nick closed the

scrapbook, put it on the table beside the bed and was about to creep out when he noticed a painting above Mr O'Hanlon's bed.

It was of a horse, golden in colour with mane and tail a creamy white. It was the horse from the newspaper photograph, there was no mistaking. Underneath the painting was a title, 'Moonglow'. Nick stared. Beauty and Grace in an act beyond Compare, the poster had said, and, as he looked at the horse, he could believe it.

He had never thought much of horses. They were all right, he supposed. But this one,

Moonglow, had been something different, he could tell.

He went downstairs, taking care not to waken Mr O'Hanlon. 'He's sleeping,' he told Mrs Thomas. 'Tell him I'll come back and see him again.'

'You do that. It cheers him up. He's not been at all well. We thought we'd lost him last month but he's a wiry old man. I'll miss him when he goes.'

'Please don't say that,' Nick said.

'It'll come to it one day, Nick. But not yet awhile, not yet. Come back and see him.'

'Tell him I will.' He walked slowly home, wondering about the horse Moonglow. And that night, before he went to sleep, he thought of it again. What had happened to it? Was it still alive, grazing happily in a paddock somewhere? But it could not be. In the photograph Mr O'Hanlon had been a young man. He was old now, fifty years older maybe. Moonglow must have died long since, he thought, and Nick felt a great sadness come over him.

What a beautiful creature it had been and how he wished he could have known it.

He went to sleep and dreamt of the horse, feeling it near. He was in the field that lay beyond the garden and when something nuzzled at his shoulder he turned to see the horse. He found an apple in his pocket and held it out and the horse gently took it. He stroked its nose and it whinnied, a soft, friendly sound.

He woke with the sound still echoing in his mind. He got out of bed and went to the window. The moon was almost full and its silvery light shone brightly on the garden and the fields beyond. He saw something move there, a fleeting vision of gold as in his dream. For a second it seemed a horse was standing there in the long grass, then it had gone and there was nothing, no gold, only the silver light of the moon. It was all a dream.

But along the edge of the fields the grass swayed and parted as if some creature was passing through.

Then Nick heard a soft low neigh, so soft that he might have imagined it. But it was real, he knew. He had seen Moonglow, seen and heard it, and heard it now again in the hush of the night.

Chapter Three

When he woke it was to the memory of a golden horse nuzzling against him. He could not make sense of it. He thought of asking Anna what she thought about it. But she would not believe him. No one would, except perhaps Mr O'Hanlon. He decided he would go and see the old man later that day, after tea.

It did not work out. His mother kept him busy doing odd jobs and by the time he had finished, clouds had gathered and rain had begun to fall.

'We're in for one of those summer storms,' his father said when he came home from work. 'The wind is getting up. It's going to be a rough old night.'

As he spoke there was a flash of lightning. It was quite a long way off for Nick counted sixteen before the roll of thunder came.

'I wanted to go and see Mr O'Hanlon,' he said.

'Not tonight, Nick. You'd get soaked,' his

mother said. 'You can go with me at the weekend.'

When Nick went to bed rain beat against the window. He stood looking out but there was nothing to be seen. Then another flash of lightning showed the garden bright and clear and, for that instant, the golden horse was there. Blackness returned and the horse was gone. He rubbed his eyes, peered out into the night and opened his window to see better.

'What on earth do you think you're doing?' He had not heard his mother come in. She closed the window.

'I thought I saw something,' he said.

'What?'

But he couldn't say and when his mother made him get into bed and tucked him in, he felt so warm and cosy that he soon went to sleep.

Lightning flashed and thunder rolled, far off at first but drawing nearer and nearer.

Nick slept, unaware of the storm, deaf to the sounds outside. Then, suddenly, the drumming of horses' hooves filled the room, pounded against the walls, echoing back and forth. He put his head under the blankets to deaden the sound but it made no difference. Ten wild black horses, maddened with fear, nostrils flaring, came charging towards him. He covered his head with his arms to protect himself and trembled. He felt the wind as the horses passed, and the thunderous beat of their hooves deafened him. He screamed as the biggest of them reared above him and came down, missing him by a breath.

An arm held him and he opened his eyes to see his mother. His father stood beside her, looking down at him with concern.

'What is it?' his father said.

'Horses. They're here.' He seemed to see and hear them still, galloping away into the distance.

'Horses?' his mother said.

'What horses?' said his father.

But he couldn't explain. He didn't know.

Lightning lit the room and a crack of thunder followed, so near it shook the house.

'Weather like this is enough to give anyone nightmares,' Nick's father said. 'And the thunder does sound like horses galloping. That must be what it was.'

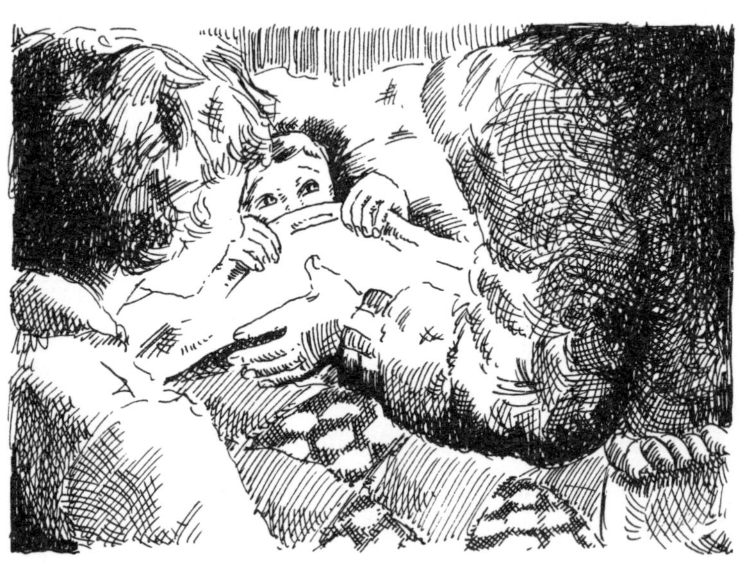

'Yes,' said Nick's mother. 'I expect that's it. Are you all right now?' she asked and bent to tuck him up again.

He was all right but he could not get to sleep. He could still see them, ten black horses running together, frightened by the storm, neighing loudly in their terror.

Slowly the sight and sound of them faded from his mind as the storm lessened. Soon even the rain ceased and quiet came. Nick slept.

When he looked from his window in the morning he saw the garden was littered with broken branches. The roof of the garden shed had been torn off. The grass in the fields was flattened as if trampled by a herd of wild horses.

Chapter Four

On Saturday Anna asked him to go with her to
the stables but he wanted to see Mr O'Hanlon.

'Why?' Anna said. 'Horses are much more
interesting than an old man.'

'I promised,' said Nick. But it wasn't just
that. Nick wanted to ask him about
Moonglow, wanted to hear his stories about
the circus.

Nick's mother was going to look after Mr
O'Hanlon while Mrs Thomas went to spend
the day with her sister, so Nick went with his
mother.

'Don't let him bother you,' Mrs Williams
said to Mr O'Hanlon. 'Send him packing if he
gets on your nerves.'

'He'll not do that,' Mr O'Hanlon said. ''Tis
glad I am to see him.' He was still in bed, but
sitting up, bright and cheerful.

'That was dirty weather we had the other
night,' he said. 'Did you enjoy it?'

'It blew the top off our garden shed.'

'Ah, 'twas nothing, nothing at all,' the old man said. 'You should have been with us the night the Big Top almost blew. A storm to end all storms, so it was. I can still see it, still hear it, the way the canvas flapped and slapped and cracked and roared and bellowed and screamed. That was a storm. More than a garden shed was lost that night, much more.' He closed his eyes, as if to see his memory more clearly, then opened them again and stared at Nick and seemed surprised to see him there.

'I'm sorry,' he said. 'For a moment I was

taken back all those years. That night everyone grabbed a rope, a pole, a guy, anything to hold on to, to stop the tent flying off into the dark. It was a struggle, I tell you, the tempest on one side, men and women on the other. Boys too. There were one or two no older than you. Everybody counted. We won in the end. That part of the fight anyway. Got the Big Top safely down, rolled and stacked. Nothing lost, except . . .' He cleared his throat. ''Tis a story to be told and I'll tell it to you some time, so I will, but not now. Some time. If you're interested, that is?'

'Oh, yes,' said Nick. 'And about Moonglow.'

'Moonglow?' said Mr O'Hanlon. 'Ah, Moonglow.' He glanced round at the painting above his bed. 'She was everything to me, Moonglow, the prettiest and daintiest of creatures, but with a will of her own. Grace and Beauty . . .'

'Beyond compare,' said Nick.

The old man beamed with pleasure. 'That's what we said and true it was.' He frowned. 'That night. The storm. It was this time of

year very nearly, mid summer. It was always a good time here in Cornwall, with the locals and the holiday-makers. We were booked here in Kenwyn for three days. The first two were a sell-out. It was the horses. Their fame had spread. No group like them anywhere, not in the whole world I reckon. That night, the last of our stay, the storm began early. The horses were nervous, on edge, made us all uneasy.' He paused, seemed to find it difficult to breathe.

'It's got to me, this pneumonia.' He tried to sit up to take a sip from a glass beside his bed.

Nick's mother appeared at the door and showed concern. 'Don't let him tire you. It's time you went, Nick.'

Mr O'Hanlon looked disappointed. 'I wanted to tell him,' he began to say but was interrupted by a fit of coughing.

'You should rest now,' Nick's mother said. 'He'll come and see you another day. It's the school holidays so he can come any time.'

Nick wanted to object, but he knew when his mother meant business. He got up but turned to Mr O'Hanlon. 'Can I borrow the scrapbook?' he said. 'I'll look after it.'

The old man smiled and nodded. 'It's by the window. Take good care of it. It holds a lot of memories.'

Nick lay in bed turning the pages of the scrapbook, searching for references to O'Hanlon's Equestrian Ballet and especially to Moonglow. He came to the last page of the book and read, 'Of all the acts of this well-loved circus the performance of the horses got the biggest applause. And the star of the troupe was the dainty, sure-footed little Palomino called Moonglow. She stole everyone's heart.' The cutting was from their own local paper and was dated fifty-three years earlier. There was nothing after that.

He fell asleep with the scrapbook still open on his bed and did not stir when his mother came in and took it from him.

He was wakened by the moon. A clear silvery light streamed in, making every detail of the room as sharp as in daylight. The downstairs clock struck two. It was the middle of the night but he felt wide awake.

He lay in bed thinking about Mr O'Hanlon and his horses, but he heard a whinny outside,

just below his bedroom window. He got quickly out of bed, went to the window, opened it wide and leaned out. There below, cropping the grass of the garden, was the golden horse. It raised its head and nickered, as if to say 'Hi!'.

'Hi!' Nick whispered in answer. He put a jacket on over his pyjamas and slipped trainers on his feet. He opened his bedroom door quietly and crept from his room, past his parents' bedroom. At the top of the stairs, away from the moonlight, it seemed suddenly dark and he stumbled. He held on to the stair rail and stood, not daring to move, afraid he might have disturbed his parents.

It was all right. The house was quiet, not a murmur, but from outside he heard the horse, pawing at the kitchen door.

He went down to the kitchen and opened the back door. There it was, the golden horse, plain to see, its creamy-white mane falling over its neck.

'Moonglow,' Nick said and the horse came nearer and lifted its head up and down as if to give Nick some message or other. He thought it was trying to come into the house but he could not allow that. He wanted to keep the secret of the horse to himself. His parents would not understand.

He guessed it wanted some little treat. He went to a cupboard and found a packet of sugar lumps. He put several in his hand and held them out to the horse. It took them gently from his palm. It tickled as the horse's lips, soft and moist, touched him. 'You are real,' he said. 'I can touch and stroke you.' He ran his hand along the horse's shoulder.

'Moonglow,' Nick said again. It was Moonglow, he was sure.

The horse turned back into the garden and Nick followed. As it bent to graze he put his arm round the horse's neck and rubbed his head against its shining golden coat. Moonlight danced on the creamy mane as the horse shook its head with pleasure.

'Moonglow,' Nick said once more. The horse twitched its ears at the sound of Nick's voice and neighed. It pushed hard against Nick, so hard that he overbalanced and, laughing, fell to the ground. Moonglow gave

another whinny, as if it saw the joke, then stood alert, ears pricked in alarm.

A light came on in Nick's bedroom and Nick looked up to see his father at the open window.

'What are you up to out there in the middle of the night?' He sounded anxious. 'Stay there till I come.' He disappeared and Nick turned to Moonglow.

There was no Moonglow, no golden horse cropping the grass. The only thing left was a sweet smell to tell him the little horse had been there.

His father arrived and helped him to his feet. 'Have you been sleep-walking, I wonder? Is that it?'

'No,' said Nick. 'I thought I heard something.'

'What sort of thing?' It was his mother now, as anxious as his father.

He couldn't tell them. They would never understand. Perhaps he had been sleep-walking, had come out here into the garden while he was dreaming. But he could still feel the touch of Moonglow's lips on the palm of his hand, slightly damp where it had taken the

sugar lumps from him. And when they went
back into the house the packet of sugar was
still on the table.

His mother looked at it, then at him.
'They're bad for your teeth,' she said and put
the packet back in the cupboard.

His parents looked at each other and shook
their heads over their son's strange behaviour.
Nick thought it was all quite clear really. He
had seen, touched and fed sugar to a horse
called Moonglow, a horse that was once the
star of O'Hanlon's Circus. He didn't know
how that could be, but it was so and he would
tell Mr O'Hanlon about it when he saw him.

His father led him back to bed. 'And don't
move from there till morning,' he warned.

Nick lay in bed and tried to make sense of
what he had seen. Perhaps the golden horse
was not Moonglow, perhaps it was a horse
from the riding stables. He hadn't ever seen
one like it, but they might have got a new one,
a Palomino. Tomorrow he would go with
Anna to the stables and see.

'But it is Moonglow,' he said sleepily to
himself. 'I just know it is.'

Chapter Five

When he woke Nick had a clear picture in his mind of a golden horse, with a flowing white mane and a long white tail. He had seen it. It had come into their garden.

It must be one of the riding stable ponies. He went next door to see Anna to ask if he could go to the stables with her.

'Of course,' she said. She was pleased he was showing an interest in horses.

'Why have you changed your mind?' Anna asked as they walked to the stables. 'What's made you want to know about horses?'

He didn't answer. He would tell her later.

The land to the stables crossed a ford. After the storm of the other night there was a lot of water in it. Two of the horses from the stables were drinking from the stream. A girl was in charge of them.

'This is a friend of mine, Josie,' Anna said. 'His name's Nick. He wants to see the horses.'

The girl smiled at Nick and waved him on to

the stables which were a few yards up the lane. Anna showed him round. There were nine horses, not one of them like Moonglow.

'Is this all?' Nick said. 'Are there any others in a paddock somewhere?'

Josie had joined them. 'This is the lot,' she said. 'They're all good mounts.' She looked him up and down. 'There are one or two ponies just right for you.'

'I wasn't thinking of riding,' he said 'I was looking for a Palomino.'

Josie opened her eyes wide. 'Oh, want something special, do we?' She was amused.

Nick had to explain, but could not give away the whole secret. 'I've seen a golden horse with a white mane and tail.'

'Yes. That sounds like a Palomino,' said Josie. 'Where have you seen it?'

Nick was uneasy. 'In a painting,' he said.

'Oh, well,' said Josie. 'We only deal in real horses here.' She laughed. 'He's a funny one, your friend, isn't he Anna?'

'No,' said Nick. 'I'm serious. I have seen one, grazing in a field near us. I thought you might have got a new horse, or that one had escaped from its owner.'

'We'd know if that was the case,' Josie said. 'And we know all the horses round about, from the Pony Shows. There's no Palomino. I can tell you that. Though, come to think of it, I have heard stories, rumours of a golden horse seen roaming the lanes some nights, but I'd have heard if any horse was missing. And I'd certainly hear if anyone had a Palomino. They're worth a lot. Lovely horses.'

'Are you staying, Nick?' Anna said. 'You could help me to muck out.'

'I've someone to see,' he answered and

turned away.

'Tell me if you find your Palomino,' Josie called after him. 'I'd like to know.' As Nick walked away he heard Anna and Josie laughing together as if they found him amusing.

He called in at home to tell his mother he was going to see Mr O'Hanlon.

'Don't stay too long,' she said. 'He gets very tired these days.'

But Mr O'Hanlon was looking very much better and was delighted to see Nick. He was still in bed.

'Sure, 'tis nonsense keeping me to my bed,'

he said. 'Don't you tell them, Nick, but I get up and walk about every once in a while.'

Nick could not keep his eyes from the painting above Mr O'Hanlon's head, the painting of Moonglow. It was Moonglow he had seen, he was sure. There was no mistaking the horse.

'What is it?' Mr O'Hanlon had seen his interest in the painting.

'Moonglow,' Nick said. 'I think I've seen a horse just like her.'

'There was never a horse like her. Sit down. I'll tell you.' He became thoughtful. 'I told you about the night of the great wind, when we nearly lost the Big Top. We lost something else that night, something more precious than the tent.' He closed his eyes and clasped his hands. 'We lost Moonglow. 'Twas the most terrible night of my life. The horses were all fenced off, in a paddock behind the Big Top. They'd finished their first act, only had the finale to come, the best part of the performance, when the gale blew so strong we had to abandon the show. The howling of the wind and the flapping of the canvas must have terrified the horses and made them bolt. We were too busy getting the Big Top safely down to notice at the time. Afterwards we found the paddock fence blown down and the horses gone. All of them — gone. There was nothing we could do that night.' He sighed.

Nick waited and the old man at last took on the story.

'At dawn the next day we went to look for them. The storm had blown itself out. It was a beautiful morning, I remember, everything smelling fresh after the rain. We found them, all the Arabs — our black horses — grazing peacefully together in a field only a few hundred yards away. But there was no Moonglow, no sight or sound of her.'

'She'd gone?' Nick said.

'She'd gone. The circus went on to its next town and I stayed behind in Kenwyn to look for her. I advertised a reward, but no one claimed it. I spent days wandering around, asking questions. No one knew a thing.'

He turned his head to look at the painting. 'That was all I had left of her and I was heart-broken.'

'What could have happened to her?'

'Who knows? Someone must have caught her. I thought gypsies might have found her. But I had good friends among them. They would have told me. She had gone, vanished into thin air.'

'What did you do?'

'I couldn't stay in Kenwyn for ever, now, could I? The circus depended on me, so it did. I caught up with it and kept it together for a year. But, without Moonglow, the pleasure of it had gone. 'Twas not the same, not for me at any rate. And I wanted to come back here, to where Moonglow was, I was sure.'

He stopped to sip at a glass of water.

'Mum said I wasn't to tire you,' Nick said. 'I'd better go.'

'No, not yet. I'm all right. They make too much of a fuss, your mother and Mrs Thomas. You do me good. I've not talked of Moonglow to anyone for years.'

'It makes you sad,' Nick said. 'It makes me sad too.'

'Yes,' said the old man. 'She was a proud horse, the daintiest, noblest creature that ever was. Loved me. Would work only for me. I don't suppose whoever took her was able to do anything with her. You'd have loved her too, I can see that.'

'I . . .' Nick began, but the old man had gone on.

'I sold up the circus, came back here, bought a plot of land and built my house where the Big Top had been. I thought if Moonglow ever came back I wanted to be here to meet her. She never did come back. I never found her. And it's too late now.'

Perhaps not, thought Nick. He wanted to tell the old man that Moonglow was back, but

did not know how to make him believe.

'I've seen her,' he blurted out.

The old man smiled. 'I see her too, in my dreams, often, that sweet golden horse. Just in my dreams.'

But it was more than a dream, Nick knew.

'I've seen her,' he said. 'Really. Fed her some sugar lumps.'

The old man smiled. 'Poor Moonglow. She's long dead, Nick. Horses are not so long-lived as humans. Doesn't seem right, that. They're much nicer than people. We're the ones who ought to die young. No, Nick, she's long dead. I wish I knew how, and where, but I'll never know now.'

'I've seen her,' Nick said doggedly.

'I wish I could believe you,' the old man said and lay back on his pillows. 'I think you'd better go now. I want to rest, but I'm glad you came.'

Nick got up to leave but at the door he turned to look back at the painting of the golden horse. There was never a horse like her, Mr O'Hanlon had said. It was true. There was only one Moonglow and he had seen her.

Chapter Six

Nick pretended to be asleep when his mother came in to to see him. He heard her moving about, tidying up after him. She was always telling him to hang his clothes up properly. But this time he had left them at the end of his bed on purpose. He intended to get up in the night, get dressed and go out into the field.

He heard his mother open a cupboard. She was putting his things away and he was annoyed. She might hear him later when he opened it. He'd have to go out in his pyjamas instead of getting dressed.

He tried to keep awake until his parents had come to bed, but failed. When he woke up he was not sure what time it was but thought it must be late. He went to his bedroom window and saw the moon, large and bright, casting its silvery light over the garden and into the field.

He put trainers on and crept downstairs. The back door was bolted but he managed to open it without making too much noise.

The night was warm so that it did not matter he was wearing only pyjamas. He heard an owl screech and a fox bark. Sounds of traffic came from the town, but here, on the edge of the country, in the old circus field, it was quiet.

He opened the gate into the field and stepped through. He hoped the golden horse would be there to meet him, but was disappointed. He looked around him. Nothing. On the other side of the fields he could see Mr O'Hanlon's house, with a light coming from one of the upstairs rooms. That would be Mr

O'Hanlon's bedroom, he supposed. Perhaps the old man was at his window looking for Moonglow too.

He was moving back towards the garden when he heard a rustling in the grass behind. He looked round and saw a movement, a stirring of the air. Something was there, but not something he could touch, or even see for certain. One moment it was there, the next it was gone.

He heard the rustling again and saw the grass shift. He turned round and round, trying to catch sight of whatever it was. Always he was too late. He felt there was something near but could see nothing definite.

It was his imagination running away with him, he decided.

Then, out of the air in front of him, a shape appeared, first thin and vague, then slowly firm and real, real and golden, the horse, Moonglow.

'Moonglow?' he said and felt her nose nudge him. She snorted, kicked her hind legs, leaping as if glad he could see her and scampered off a few yards away from him. He followed her,

caught up with her and put his arm round her neck. She let him hold her.

'I've heard all about you,' he said. 'From Mr O'Hanlon.'

The horse shivered, whinnied and bent her head. Then she moved, walking away from Nick, towards the building on the other side of the field where the light shone from Mr O'Hanlon's bedroom window.

'What do you want?' Nick asked.

The horse raised its head, whinnied and reared on its hind legs exactly as he had seen her do in the photograph.

'I know,' Nick said, and was sure he did. Moonglow wanted him to tell Mr O'Hanlon that she was there, that she had come back.

'Wait here,' he said. 'I'll tell him.'

He ran across towards the house, through the gate into the garden, round to the front door and rang the bell. He rang again and again, impatiently.

The door opened an inch or two and a very suspicious Mrs Thomas peered at him through the crack.

'Good heavens!' she said when she recognised him 'What on earth is the matter?'

'I must see him,' Nick said. 'I must.'

'Mr O'Hanlon? You can't. He's not to be disturbed.'

'It's important. Please.'

'Bless my soul! You're in your pyjamas! Come in. I'll give your mother a ring.'

'I must see him, I tell you.'

Mrs Thomas looked at him as if he was mad. 'Come in here,' she said and led him into a large room filled with old-fashioned furniture. 'Sit down. Stay there while I telephone your mother.' She closed the door and Nick heard her pick up the telephone and speak. Then he heard her put the telephone down and move away. He went quietly to the door and peeped out. She was going upstairs, to see Mr O'Hanlon, he supposed. He closed the door and waited.

When she came back she said, 'Mr O'Hanlon's not to be disturbed. You don't seem to know how ill he is. Why do you want to see him anyway?'

'I've got a message for him.'

'A message? Who from?'

'From . . .' He stopped. What could he say? From a horse? The ghost of a horse? Mrs Thomas would be certain he was mad then.

'Let me see him. Please.'

There was a ring at the door and Mrs Thomas went to answer it. Nick seized his chance and ran to the foot of the stairs but Mrs Thomas had guessed his intention and caught hold of him.

'What's going on?' It was Nick's father. 'What are you doing here, Nick?'

'And in your pyjamas!' his mother exclaimed. 'I don't believe it. Really, Nick. Have you been sleep-walking again?'

Nick didn't answer. He knew he wouldn't be allowed to see Mr O'Hanlon now. He pretended he was confused as if he had been sleep-walking.

'I'm sorry for all the trouble,' Nick's mother said to Mrs Thomas. 'I can't think what's got into the boy.'

'He was thinking of Mr O'Hanlon, I expect. He's worried about him. We all are. I don't think it'll be long now.'

Nick looked at her and then at his father

who put an arm around him.

'I wanted to tell him something,' he said. 'It's important.'

'Tomorrow,' Mrs Thomas said. 'Come tomorrow — or is it already today? If he's well enough you can see him then.'

His parents took him home and his father stayed with him until he was sure his son was asleep. Nick wished he could tell him what he had seen. Surely someone would believe him, surely someone would understand how important it was to tell Mr O'Hanlon that Moonglow had come back.

Chapter Seven

Nick was not allowed to go to see Mr O'Hanlon the next day. 'He's not well enough to have visitors,' his mother said.

I've got news that will cheer him up, Nick thought. He will want to hear about Moonglow.

'Perhaps you'll be able to see him tomorrow,' his mother said.

When Anna called for him he went with her to the stables. Josie said 'Have you found your Palomino yet?' and laughed.

He wanted to say, 'Yes, I have found her,' but he knew Josie would not believe him.

'I have found her,' he whispered to Anna when Josie had gone.

'A Palomino?'

'Yes. A horse called Moonglow.' He had to tell someone.

'Where?' She was excited. 'I've never seen a Palomino. Only read about them.'

'Promise you won't laugh?'

'Why should I laugh?' She was busy raking straw out of one of the stalls. Nick took a fork and helped her.

'Don't tell anyone else.'

Anna stopped work and looked at him.

'I can keep a secret. Try me.'

'It's a ghost,' he said and was sorry he'd spoken.

Anna hooted with laughter. 'A ghost! Of a horse!'

'Shh,' he said. 'I don't want Josie to hear.'

'You're serious,' Anna said. 'You think you have seen a ghost, a Palomino ghost. Well, I don't believe it. I don't believe in ghosts anyway.'

'Neither do I,' said Nick. 'But I've seen her.'

He heard Josie coming and put his finger to his lips to tell Anna to say nothing.

'Would you like to have a ride sometime?' Josie said.

Nick shook his head.

'Oh, I forgot,' Josie said. 'You're only interested in Palominos. I'll have to see if we can find one for you. Perhaps we'll catch the one that's been seen the last few nights.'

'A Palomino?' Anna said, looking at Nick.

'No one seems quite sure. It appears, then vanishes before anyone can get hold of it. Very elusive, it is.' She smiled at Nick. 'I meant it. You can have a free ride whenever you want.'

'Someday,' he said.

He and Anna walked home together.

'Where did you see the horse?' Anna said.

'In the field outside our garden. Late at night, it was. After everyone was asleep.'

'You really did see something?'

'Honestly. I expect you would if you watched with me.'

'What time?'

'I don't know. After midnight, I expect.'

'I'll come if I can creep past Emily without waking her.' Emily was Anna's younger sister. 'Twelve o'clock tonight?'

'I'll be there,' Nick said. 'In the field, just after midnight.'

He was determined to keep awake until he heard the clock strike twelve, but he went to sleep. When he woke he did not know what time it was but something had disturbed him. He lay for a moment trying to think what he was supposed to be doing when he heard a noise, the noise that had wakened him. It was a rattle of pebbles against his bedroom window.

He went to see what it was. Anna was standing below, beckoning him. He waved to show he was coming down.

He opened his bedroom door and was creeping downstairs when he heard his mother's voice.

'What was that?' she said, and he heard the light in his parents' bedroom go on.

'I'll go and see,' his father sleepily replied.

'Be careful, dear,' his mother said.

Nick stood still, not daring to move, afraid of giving himself away.

His father came out of the bedroom and stood uncertainly at the top of the stairs. Nick pressed himself against the wall, hoping to escape notice.

'What is it, George?' his mother called.

Nick's father switched the landing light on, looked down and saw Nick.

'It's you again!' he said. 'It's Nick,' he called to his wife. 'Only Nick.'

'What on earth!' his mother exclaimed as she came out of the bedroom, wrapping a dressing-gown about her. She hurried to him and put her arm around him. 'What is it this time, Nick? Is something worrying you?'

How could he explain? He allowed himself to be led back to bed. His mother tucked the blankets tightly round him and stood, with his father, looking down at him. He could tell they were anxious about him, but there was no reason to be.

And what of Anna? He expected she had got fed up with waiting for him.

He wished his parents would leave him but they seemed determined to stay till he had fallen asleep. He turned over and gave a light snore, pretending to be asleep.

He heard his mother say. 'I guess he's worried about poor Mr O'Hanlon. I know he's fond of the old man.'

It's not that, Nick wanted to say, not really, but he was too sleepy to say anything, too sleepy to be aware when his parents left him to go back to their own room.

Chapter Eight

'Can I go to see Mr O'Hanlon today?' Nick asked his mother.

'You can come as far as the house with me and then we'll see.'

Mrs Thomas greeted them with the news that Mr O'Hanlon was feeling chirpier. 'I don't suppose it would hurt if you saw him for a few minutes. But you mustn't stay too long.'

Mr O'Hanlon raised his hand to greet Nick. He was looking very frail. He spoke slowly as if it was difficult for him to get his breath.

'I'm glad you came,' he said.

'I wanted to see you two nights ago,' Nick said.

'Pass me the painting,' the old man said. 'Of Moonglow.'

Nick stretched over and unhooked the painting. He gave it to Mr O'Hanlon who looked at it for a long moment and then let it fall to the bed.

'No horse was ever like this one. Proud.' He

66

paused for breath. 'Would bow the knee to no one, not even to me.' Nick wanted to tell him about seeing Moonglow, but the old man was trying to speak. 'Loved me, she did. And I loved her. Have looked for her. Never found her. Too late now.' He sighed. 'Thought I saw her the other night. A dream, that's all. Nothing but dreams left now. Saw Seamus and Sean too, grumpy as ever.' He chuckled softly and then coughed, catching his breath. He pointed to his bedside table and Nick passed him a glass of water. The old man sipped it and lay back, closing his eyes.

'I've seen her,' Nick said.

The old man's eyes opened. 'You?'

'Yes. It wasn't a dream.'

'I wish I could believe you.'

'Outside, in the field at the end of your garden. In the moonlight. She knew you were here.'

'Moonglow?'

'I know it was her. She wanted me to tell you.'

Mr O'Hanlon picked up the painting again and stared at it. 'Just as I remember her. And all I have left of her.' He was talking to himself. He seemed to have forgotten Nick was there.

Nick sat quietly until Mr O'Hanlon said, 'You can hang it up again.' Nick did as he was told. He wanted to ask Mr O'Hanlon more about the circus but the old man's eyes had closed. He was snoring gently. Nick crept out and went downstairs.

Anna was waiting for him at home. 'What happened to you last night?' she said crossly.

'Dad caught me. I couldn't get out.'

'Parents!' she said. 'They're all the same.'

'Did you see anything?' he asked.

'Of course not. There's nothing to see.' She was still cross. 'I don't believe there ever was a horse.'

'That's all right,' said Nick. 'Believe what you want. It doesn't change things.'

'We could go again tonight,' she said.

'I thought you didn't believe me.'

'It's fun anyway — if you don't keep me waiting half the night. Midnight again?'

'Midnight, I promise,' Nick said.

This time he kept awake until he heard the clock downstairs strike twelve. He crept quietly to his parents' bedroom door and listened. He could hear his father snoring. He stepped warily on every stair, hoping they wouldn't creak. At last he managed to get out of the house and there was still no sound from his parents. He sighed with relief.

Anna was already in the field.

'I thought you were going to be late again,' she said. 'I've brought two pieces of cake to eat. We might have to wait a long time.'

It was dark, with the moon again hidden behind clouds. 'It's too dark to see anything, even a ghost,' said Anna, but Nick wasn't listening to her.

'Quiet!' he said. 'Did you hear?'

There was a rustling in the grass.

'It's only a rabbit,' Anna said.

'Wait,' he said.

A sound of hooves, trotting through the field, came to them, then a gentle whinny.

'Did you hear that?' Anna said in a low voice, as if she did not believe her ears. 'Can you see anything?'

Nick felt the nudge of a horse's nose at his shoulder, turned but could see nothing.

'Here,' he said. 'She's here.' But the touch had gone.

'There's nothing there,' Anna said. 'But I did hear a horse, I'm sure.'

'Stay still. She'll come back,' Nick said.

'Look, over there,' Anna said sharply. 'I'm sure I saw something.' The moon shone briefly through the clouds and in its light Nick caught a glimpse of gold, no sooner seen than gone.

'Was it her?' Anna said. 'Is that all you see or hear?'

'No,' Nick said. 'I've stroked her, fed her sugar lumps.'

'She's gone now.'

They stood for several minutes hoping for another sight of the horse, but Nick knew she would not return that night. Perhaps she would not come while Anna was there. Perhaps Moonglow only trusted him. Maybe he should have kept her appearance secret, even from Anna.

'Tomorrow night?' Anna said. 'Shall we try again?'

Chapter Nine

It was almost dark when Anna came round. They had agreed to start their watch for Moonglow earlier and to take it in turns to look out and to watch from inside the house to begin with. Anna still did not quite believe in the horse. 'I'll keep watch,' she said. 'But I don't expect to see anything.'

Nick knew what he had seen and didn't really care if Anna believed him or not, but he hoped Moonglow would show herself tonight. He did not know why tonight was specially important but it was.

Nick's mother appeared looking anxious. 'I've just had a message about Mr O'Hanlon. He's taken a turn for the worse. I must go round and see him, do what I can.'

'Tell him . . .' Nick began, but he didn't know what he wanted to say to Mr O'Hanlon, just that he understood the magic of Moonglow, knew why the memory of the horse meant so much to the old man.

'I'll tell him,' his mother said. 'I know what you want to say. You'll miss him, won't you?'

Nick didn't like to think of not seeing Mr O'Hanlon ever again. Knowing each other had meant a great deal to both of them.

He gave his attention to the scrapbook, looking again at the many photographs of Moonglow and especially those which showed Mr O'Hanlon and the horse together. He left it to Anna to stand at the window and keep a look-out.

'There's nothing,' she said after a while. 'She's not going to come. I don't believe there ever was a horse.'

'Change places,' Nick said. 'I'll watch.'

He went to the window and stood for a while, looking into the dark. The moon had not yet risen. When it did he was sure Moonglow would appear.

Then he saw the moon, over the trees, partly covered by racing clouds, so that it seemed to be sailing through the sky. And, as the silver light touched the hedge at the end of the garden, he saw Moonglow. She was standing alert, ears pricked, her head to one side, as if listening for something.

'She's there,' Nick whispered. 'come and see.'

Anna joined him. The moonlight went and came and went again.

'Did you see her?' Nick asked.

Anna did not answer for a long time, then she said, 'She's beautiful. The most beautiful horse that ever was.'

The moon shone and Moonglow lifted her head and whinnied.

'Come,' said Nick and led Anna to the back door and into the garden.

'You'll frighten her,' she said.

'She's waiting for me, you'll see. She knows me. She knows who I am.'

They walked slowly through the garden and stood at the gate with Moonglow looking over at them. She put her head forward to be stroked by Anna. Anna whispered to the horse saying over and over again, 'Moonglow, Moonglow.'

Moonglow nodded her head several times and rubbed against Anna.

They opened the gate into the field and joined the horse.

'Will she let me ride her?' Anna said.

'No,' Nick said. 'Don't try. No one but Mr O'Hanlon ever rode her.'

At the sound of the old man's name the horse shivered, its flanks rippling in the moonlight. She set off suddenly across the field, leapt over the stream which separated the field from the meadows behind Mr O'Hanlon's house, and galloped away. Nick and Anna followed but could not keep pace with her.

'Where's she gone?' Anna said and, for a moment, Nick thought the horse had vanished.

Then he saw her. She had stopped to graze just a few yards from where the old man's garden began. When Anna and Nick drew near she paid no attention. From time to time she raised her head to look up at the house, then, with a shake of her mane, settled to graze again.

Nick stood beside her, and rested his hand on Moonglow's neck. There was something so real and solid and strong about the creature. It wasn't possible she was a ghost. But she was. At any moment the horse would go, just vanish into thin air.

There was a light in Mr O'Hanlon's bed-room. The curtains were drawn over the win-dow and shadows moved behind it. Nick thought he recognised the silhouette of his mother, and there was another figure, Doctor Taylor perhaps.

He felt a shiver pass through Moonglow. The horse raised her head and gave a soft neigh, a long slow call as if speaking to someone. Then she shook her mane, reared up on her hind legs, her front legs pawing the air. Nick stood away and watched as Moonglow lowered her front legs to the ground and stood for a moment gazing at the lighted window. Then slowly she lowered her head and sank to her knees, bowing. She stayed kneeling for a whole minute, then got to her feet, lifted her nose to the air, braced her legs, turned and swept so swiftly past Nick and Anna that they saw nothing, felt only a rush of air and heard, far off, a whinny of farewell.

'Where's she gone?' Anna exclaimed.

'She's left us.' Nick knew she had gone for good. He thought he heard the sound of

hooves across the field, but this time it was his imagination at work, he knew.

'You saw her?' he said.

'I touched her. She was there. She was real. And so very beautiful.'

They went to Mr O'Hanlon's garden and round to the front of the house. They were going into the road to turn for home when the door of the house opened and Nick's mother appeared at the top of the steps.

'Is that you?' she said in surprise when she caught sight of Nick.

'We saw . . .' Anna began. Nick caught hold of her arm to stop her giving away their secret.

But Nick's mother hadn't heard.

'I'm sorry, Nick,' she said. 'Mr O'Hanlon died, a few minutes ago. Don't be upset.'

'I'm not,' Nick said. Mr O'Hanlon and Moonglow had found each other. That was nothing to be upset about.

'He said you were to have the painting of the golden horse. He said you cared.' She turned to go back into the house. 'I've got more to do here. Tell your father what's happened. Get off home and get to bed. It's late.'

Before getting into bed that evening he stood at his window looking out on the garden and the fields, hoping for another glimpse of Moonglow but, though the moon shone brightly over the landscape, there was no sign of the horse, no flash of gold. But, just before he went to sleep, he thought he heard a whinny.

'Moonglow,' he sighed. But there was no answer. This time the horse had gone for good.